W.C. Bennett

Baby May

SALZWASSER
VERLAG

W.C. Bennett

Baby May

Reprint of the original, first published in 1859.

1st Edition 2022 | ISBN: 978-3-37512-446-5

Verlag (Publisher): Salzwasser Verlag GmbH, Zeilweg 44, 60439 Frankfurt, Deutschland
Vertretungsberechtigt (Authorized to represent): E. Roepke, Zeilweg 44, 60439 Frankfurt, Deutschland
Druck (Print): Books on Demand GmbH, In de Tarpen 42, 22848 Norderstedt, Deutschland

BABY MAY,

AND

OTHER POEMS ON INFANTS.

BY

W. C. BENNETT.

LONDON:
CHAPMAN AND HALL, 193, PICCADILLY.
1859.

TO

WILLIAM FREDERICK ROCK,

THIS LITTLE VOLUME

Is Inscribed,

WITH THE WARMEST ESTEEM AND REGARD,

BY HIS FRIEND,

W. C. BENNETT.

2, THE CIRCUS,
GREENWICH.

CONTENTS.

PREFACE.

TEN years since, "Baby May" was printed for private circulation; and I shortly after received a request from the late Mr. Douglas Jerrold that he might give it to the public in his "Shilling Magazine." It at once became a favourite. Since then it has been a pleasure to me to know that the little lady has made friends far and near, both in England and America; among whom she reckons with becoming pride, among the dead, Mary Russell Mitford, who re-introduced her to the public in her "Recollections of a Literary Life,"—among the living, Mr. John Ruskin, Mr. Nathaniel Hawthorne, Mr. and Mrs. Howitt, and many of the leading writers of England and America. The volume in which I published this best known of my poems is out of print, but I find that "Baby May" still holds her place in the recollections of her old acquaintances, and year

by year gains new ones. It is recited in lectures,
and included in American selections from the
English poets ; and now I hear of constant
requests that this and other poems of mine, on
kindred subjects, may be reprinted at a price
which will enable the many who wish for them
to obtain them. So I again present her to the
world, with a confident hope that her welcome
may be as warm an one as that which so long
since greeted her on her first appearance.

BABY MAY.

CHEEKS as soft as July peaches,
   Lips whose dewy scarlet teaches
Poppies paleness—round large eyes .
Ever great with new surprise,
Minutes filled with shadeless gladness,
Minutes just as brimmed with sadness,
Happy smiles and wailing cries,
Crows and laughs and tearful eyes,
Lights and shadows swifter born
Than on wind-swept Autumn corn,
Ever some new tiny notion
Making every limb all motion—
Catchings up of legs and arms,
Throwings back and small alarms,
Clutching fingers—straightening jerks,
Twining feet whose each toe works,
Kickings up and straining risings,
Mother's ever new surprisings,
Hands all wants and looks all wonder
At all things the heavens under,
Tiny scorns of smiled reprovings
That have more of love than lovings,
Mischiefs done with such a winning
Archness, that we prize such sinning,

B

Breakings dire of plates and glasses,
Graspings small at all that passes,
Pullings off of all that's able
To be caught from tray or table;
Silences—small meditations,
Deep as thoughts of cares for nations,
Breaking into wisest speeches
In a tongue that nothing teaches,
All the thoughts of whose possessing
Must be wooed to light by guessing;
Slumbers—such sweet angel-seemings
That we'd ever have such dreamings,
Till from sleep we see thee breaking,
And we'd always have thee waking;
Wealth for which we know no measure,
Pleasure high above all pleasure,
Gladness brimming over gladness,
Joy in care—delight in sadness,
Loveliness beyond completeness,
Sweetness distancing all sweetness,
Beauty all that beauty may be,
That's May Bennett—that's my baby.

BABY'S SHOES.

O THOSE little, those little blue shoes!
  Those shoes that no little feet use!
    O the price were high,
    That those shoes would buy,
Those little blue unused shoes!

For they hold the small shape of feet
That no more their mother's eyes meet,
    That, by God's good will,
    Years since grew still,
And ceased from their totter so sweet!

And O, since that baby slept,
So hush'd! how the mother has kept,
    With a tearful pleasure,
    That little dear treasure,
And o'er them thought and wept!

For they mind her for evermore
Of a patter along the floor,
    And blue eyes she sees
    Look up from her knees,
With the look that in life they wore.

As they lie before her there,
There babbles from chair to chair
    A little sweet face,
    That's a gleam in the place,
With its little gold curls of hair.

Then O wonder not that her heart
From all else would rather part
    Than those tiny blue shoes
    That no little feet use,
And whose sight makes such fond tears start.

TODDLING MAY.

FIVE pearly teeth and two soft blue eyes,
    Two sinless eyes of blue,
That are dim or are bright they scarce know why,
    That, baby dear, is you.
And parted hair of a pale, pale gold,
    That is priceless, every curl,
And a boldness shy, and a fear half bold,
    Ay, that's my baby girl.

A small, small frock, as the snowdrop white,
    That is worn with a tiny pride,
With a sash of blue, by a little sight
    With a baby wonder eyed;
And a pattering pair of restless shoes,
    Whose feet have a tiny fall,
That not for the world's coined wealth we'd lose,
    That, Baby May, we call.

A rocker of dolls with staring eyes
    That a thought of sleep disdain,
That with shouts of tiny lullabies
    Are by'd and by'd in vain;
A drawer of carts with baby noise,
    With strainings and pursed-up brow,
Whose hopes are cakes and whose dreams are toys,
    Ay, that's my baby now.

A sinking of heart, a shuddering dread,
    Too deep for a word or tear,
Or a joy whose measure may not be said,
    As the future is hope or fear;
A sumless venture, whose voyage's fate
    We would and yet would not know,
Is she whom we dower with love as great
    As is perilled by hearts below.

Oh what as her tiny laugh is dear,
    Or our days with gladness girds!
Or what is the sound we love to hear
    Like the joy of her baby words!
Oh pleasure our pain, and joys our fears
    Should be, could the future say,
Away with sorrow—time has no tears
    For the eyes of Baby May.

CRADLE SONGS.

1.

L ULLABY! O lullaby!
Baby, hush that little cry!
 Light is dying,
 Bats are flying,
Bees to-day with work have done;
So, till comes the morrow's sun,
Let sleep kiss those bright eyes dry!
 Lullaby! O lullaby!

Lullaby! O lullaby!
Hushed are all things, far and nigh;
 Flowers are closing,
 Birds reposing,
All sweet things with life have done,
Sweet, till dawns the morning sun,
Sleep then kiss those blue eyes dry!
 Lullaby! O lullaby!

TO A LADY I KNOW, AGED ONE.

O SUNNY curls! O eyes of blue!
  The hardest natures known,
Baby, would softly speak to you,
  With strangely tender tone;
What marvel, Mary, if from such
  Your sweetness, love would call,
We love you, baby, O how much,
  Most dear of all things small!

Unborn, how, more than all on earth,
  Your mother yearn'd to meet
Your dream'd-of face; you, from your birth,
  Most sweet of all things sweet!
Even now for your small hands' first press
  Of her full happy breast,
How oft does she God's goodness bless,
  And feel her heart too blest!

You came, a wonder to her eyes,
  That doated on each grace,
Each charm that still with new surprise
  She show'd us in your face:

Small beauties? ah, to her not small,
　How plain to her blest mind!
Though, baby dear, I doubt if all,
　All that she found, could find.

A year has gone, and, mother, say,
　Through all that year's blest round,
In her, has one sweet week or day
　Not some new beauty found?
What moment has not fancied one,
　Since first your eyes she met?
And, wife, I know you have not done
　With finding fresh ones yet.

Nor I; for, baby, some new charm
　Each coming hour supplies,
So sweet, we think change can but harm
　Your sweetness in our eyes,
Till comes a newer, and we know
　As that fresh charm we see,
In you, sweet Nature wills to show
　How fair a babe can be.

Kind God, that gave this precious gift,
　More clung-to every day,
To Thee our eyes we trembling lift—
　Take not Thy gift away!
Looking on her, we start in dread,
　We stay our shuddering breath,
And shrink to feel the terror said
　In that one dark word—death.

O tender eyes! O beauty strange!
　When childhood shall depart,
O that thou, babe, through every change,
　May'st keep that infant heart!
O gracious God! O this make sure,
　That, of no grace beguiled,
The woman be in soul as pure
　As now she is, a child!

THE SEASONS.

A BLUE-EYED child that sits amid the noon,
   O'erhung with a laburnum's drooping sprays,
Singing her little songs, while, softly round,
   Along the grass the chequered sunshine plays.

All beauty that is throned in womanhood,
   Pacing a summer garden's fountained walks,
That stoops to smooth a glossy spaniel down,
   To hide her flushing cheek from one who talks.

A happy mother with her fair-faced girls,
   In whose sweet Spring again her youth she sees,
With shout and dance, and laugh, and bound, and song,
   Stripping an autumn orchard's laden trees.

An aged woman in a wintry room,
   Frost on the pane—without, the whirling snow ;
Reading old letters of her far-off youth,
   Of pleasures past, and griefs of long ago.

TO A LOCKET.

CASKET of dear fancies,
  O little case of gold,
What rarest wealth of memories
  Thy tiny round will hold!
With this first curl of baby's
  In thy small charge will live
All thoughts that all her little life
  To memory can give.

O prize its silken softness,
  Within its amber round
What worlds of sweet rememberings
  Will still by us be found;
The weak, shrill cry so blessing
  The curtained room of pain,
With every since-felt feeling
  To us 'twill bring again.

'Twill mind us of her lying
  In rest soft-pillowed deep,
While, hands the candle shading,
  We stole upon her sleep,

Of many a blessed moment
  Her little rest above
We hung in marvelling stillness,
  In ecstacy of love.

'Twill mind us, radiant sunshine
  For all our shadowed days,
Of all her baby wonderings,
  Of all her little ways.
Of all her tiny shoutings,
  Of all her starts and fears,
And sudden mirths out-gleaming
  Through eyes yet hung with tears.

There's not a care—a watching—
  A hope—a laugh—a fear,
Of all her little bringing,
  But we shall find it here;
Then, tiny golden warder,
  Oh safely ever hold
This glossy silken memory,
  This little curl of gold.

CRADLE SONGS.

2.

SLEEP ! the bird is in its nest;
  Sleep ! the bee is hushed in rest;
Sleep ! rocked on thy mother's breast;
      Lullaby !
To thy mother's fond heart pressed,
      Lullaby !

Sleep ! the waning daylight dies;
Sleep ! the stars dream in the skies;
Daisies long have closed their eyes;
      Lullaby !
 Calm, how calm! on all things lies;
      Lullaby !

Sleep then, sleep! my heart's delight;
Sleep ! and through the darksome night,
Round thy bed God's angels bright,
      Lullaby !
Guard thee till I come with light;
      Lullaby !

EPITAPHS FOR INFANTS.

1.

HERE, Spring's tenderest nurslings set,
  Wind-flowers and the violet;
Here the white-drooped snowdrop frail,
And the lily of the vale;
All of sweetness passing soon,
Withering ere the year be noon;
For the little rester here,
Like these infants of the year,
Was, oh grief, as fair as they,
And as quickly fled away.

2.

Here the gusts of wild March blow
But in murmurs faint and low;
Ever here, when Spring is green,
Be the brightest verdure seen;
And when June's in field and glade,
Here be ever freshest shade.
Here hued Autumn latest stay,
Latest call the flowers away;
And when Winter's shrilling by,
Here its snows the warmest lie;
For a little life is here,
Hid in earth, for ever dear,
And this grassy heap above
Sorrow broods and weeping love.

3.

On this little grassy mound
Never be the darnel found:
Ne'er be venomed nettle seen
On this little heap of green;
For the little lost one here .
Was too sweet for aught of fear,
Aught of harm to harbour nigh •
This green spot where she must lie;
So be nought but sweetness found
On this little grassy mound.

4.

Here in gentle pity, Spring,
Let thy sweetest voices sing;
Nightingale, be here thy song
Charmed by grief to linger long;
Here the thrush with longest stay
Pipe its pleasant song to day,
And the blackbird warble shrill
All its passion latest still;
Still the old grey tower above
Her small rest, the swallow love,
And through all June's honied hours
Booming bees hum in its flowers,
And when comes the eve's cold gray
Murmuring gnats unresting play
Weave, while, round, the beetle's flight
Drones across the shadowing night;
For the sweetness dreaming here
Was a gladness to the year,
And the sad months all should bring
Dirges o'er her sleep to sing.

5.

Haunter of the opening year,
Ever be the primrose here;
Whitest daisies deck the spot,
Pansies and forget-me-not,
Fairest things that earliest fly,
Sweetness blooming but to die;
For this blossom, o'er whose fall
Sorrow sighs, was fair as all,
But, alas, as frail as they,
All as quickly fled away.

TO OUR BABY KATE.

A REVERIE.

MARVEL, baby, 'tis to me
   What thy little thoughts can be,
What the meanings small, that reach
Hearing in thy mites of speech,
Sayings that no language know
More than coo, and cry, and crow,
Would-be words, that hide away
All that they themselves would say,
Tiny fancies courting sight,
Masked from all in shrouding night;
Fain its secret I'd beguile
From the mystery of thy smile;
Fain would fathom all that lies
In thy pleasure and surprise,
In the fancies flitting through
Those two eyes of wondering blue,
In thy starts and tiny fears,
Gleams of joy and fleeting tears.
Ah, in vain I seek to win
Way to the small life within!
Curious thought no clue can find
To that wondrous world, thy mind,

That its little sights hath shown
Unto fancy's gaze alone;
Therefore do I converse hold
Oft with fancy, to unfold
All the marvels of its seeing,
Wordless mysteries of thy being;
Then of all seen things it tells
Unto thee, high miracles
How thy baby fancy lingers,
Wondering minutes o'er thy fingers,
Or, still marvelling more and more,
Eyes thy pinked feet o'er and o'er;
How the world and all things seem
Airy shadows of a dream,
Unsubstantial—forms unreal,
Out to which thy graspings feel
Wavering stretchings, marvelling much
At the mystery of a touch;
How with little shout thou'dst pass
To thy likeness in the glass,
Or thy little talks are told
Unto all thou dost behold,
Guessed-at griefs and baby joys
Crowed to busy sister's toys,
Or in murmurings low, rehearsed
To the kitten for thee nursed.
So with fancy do I dream,
Baby mine, until I seem
All the little thoughts to know,
All thy little acts below,
Till thought comes and bids me own
That I dream and dream alone.

Yet one surety lies above
Reason's doubtings—thine is love,
Love abundant, leaping out
In thy lighted look and shout,
In thy joy that sorrow dumbs,
In thy bubbling laugh that comes
Ever still with glad surprise
When thy mother meets thine eyes.
Love is in thy eager watch
Ever strained her form to catch,
In thy glance that, place to place,
Tracks the gladness of her face,
In thy hush of joy that charms
Cries to stillness in her arms,
Calms of rapture, blessing, blest,
Rosy nestlings in her breast,
Dreaming eyes for ever raising
Raptured gazes to her gazing,
Gaze so blessed, sure we deem
Heaven is in thy happy dream.
So our love would have it be
Ever, little Kate, with thee;
Treasure, treasures all above,
Ever, baby, thine be love,
Love, that doubly-mirrored lives
In the smiles it wins and gives,
Love, that gives to life its worth,
Lending glory to the earth.

ON A DEAD INFANT.

DEAD! dead!—what peace abides within the word—
  For thee, O little one, what bliss of rest!
By her who bore thee, with what anguish heard,
    God knows!—God knoweth best;
God willeth best; yet while the words we say,
We know thy grief, wild mother, must have way.

Oh, never shall those tiny fingers press
Her cheek!—oh, never to the full breasts steal,
That yearn their tender touch, that so would bless,
    Their blessed touch to feel!
Oh, never shall those closed lids opening rise
To look delight into her hungering eyes!

Yearned for—how yearned for wast thou, little one!
Each month more dear that seemed to bring thee near,
Alas! that seemed, but seemed; God's will be done!
    We may not know thee here;
We may not know thee, but as, babe, thou art,
Cold even to thy mother's quivering heart.

Not know thee! Mother, with thy sorrow wild,
How is that still face stamped within thy heart!
That face so looked on, when, " Give me my child!"
    Thou criedst, nor dared we part
In that first moment from thy arms' embrace
The cold white stillness of that blind, fixed face.

God comfort her! all human words are vain
To bid her shun to die or care to live.
Who shall bid peace to be for her again?
    Who, save God, comfort give?
Who fill the empty heart that finds a void
In all it feared or hoped for or enjoyed?

God comfort her!—who else?—not even he
Who for thee, sweet one, bore a father's love,
Who, with what pride and joy! she looked to see
    Bend this new life above,
And show her in his eyes the unshadowed bliss
That looked from hers—alas! now changed to this!

Leave her to God and to the tender years
That soften misery into gentle grief,
Grief that may almost find at last from tears,
    Sad tears, may find relief,
Grief that from time may gather perfect trust
In all Heaven wills, and own even this is just.

For thee, dead snowdrop, all our tears are dried;
We know thee evermore as to us given
Within our hearts for ever to abide,
    Type of all meet for heaven;
Type of all purity of which we guess,
That heaven shall make more pure and earth not less.

Wake not! the cruel tender hand of death,
Death, with a tenderness for earth too deep,
Ere thou hadst drawn one mortal troubled breath,
    Hushed thee to quiet sleep,
Stilled, ere it woke, the anguish of thy cries,
Nor gave the tears of earth to dim thine eyes.

Why would we wake thee?—Joy and grief, we know,
Walk hand in hand along earth's crowded ways;
Who 'scape the thorns that in our paths below
    For all life thickly lays?
Why should we wish thee on a weary way
Where thou might'st long for night while yet 'twas day?

For we, most blest, even when to heaven we turn
Eyes bright with thanks for all that makes life dear,
Even then our trembling hearts have not to learn
    Of sorrows that are here—
Of griefs that dimmed our dearest hours with tears—
Of bitter memories that seem shadowing fears.

Hope has no part in thee, in surety lost,
Sweet bud of being, but to bloom above;
Nor may our thoughts of thee with fear be crossed,
    Thou, homed in God's dear love,
Borne by thy heavenly Father's hand from all
That makes the purest stoop, the strongest fall.

Lily, thou shalt not know the soiling gust
Of earthly passion bow thee to its will;
Temptation and all ill are from thee thrust,
    Nor tears thine eyes shall fill;
Remorse and penitence thou shalt not need,
From sin's pollution and earth's errors freed.

Oh, blessed, to 'scape the mystery of life,
Its wavering walk 'twixt holiness and sin!
Allowed, without earth's struggles—our weak strife,
    Heaven's palms to win,
Through the bright portals thou at once hast pressed,
To endless blessedness and lasting rest.

CRADLE SONGS.

3.

LULLABY—lullaby, baby dear!
  Take thy rest without a fear;
Quiet sleep, for mother is here,
Ever wakeful, ever near,
    Lullaby!

Lullaby—lullaby! gone is the light,
Yet let not darkness my baby fright;
Mother is with her amid the night,
Then softly sleep, my heart's delight,
    Lullaby

May thy small dreams no ill things see,
Kind Heaven keep watch, my baby, o'er thee,
Kind angels bright thy guardians be,
And give thee smiling to day and to me,
    Lullaby!

Sleep, sleep on! thy rest is deep;
But, ah! what wild thoughts on me creep,
As by thy side my watch I keep,
To think how like to death is sleep
    Lullaby!

But God our Father will hear my prayer,
And have thee, dear one, in His care;
Thee, little one, soft breathing there,
To me the Lord's dear love will spare,
    Lullaby!

Sleep on! sleep on! till glad day break,
And with the sunshine gladly wake,
Thy mother's day, how blest! to make,
Her life, what joy! through thy dear sake,
    Lullaby!

THE WISH.

MY boy, my boy, what would I have
  Thy future lot should be,
Were that sweet fay, so kind of old,
  To leave the choice with me?
Were she to say, " My fairy power,
  To grant all blessings, use;
Give what thou wilt to this young life,
  And what thou wilt, refuse."

Her diamond wand, my little one,
  Above thee would I raise,
" Be health," I'd say, " be beauty thine,
  My boy, through all thy days.
The perfect powers that give thee strength
  Thy work on earth to do;
The perfect form, that shows the soul's
  Own beauty shining through.

" Be plenty thine; that, wealthy, thou
  Mayst independent live;
That, rich, to thee it may be given
  Abundantly to give:
That heaven, through means of that thou hast,
  To thee may be made sure;
In life—in death—that thou mayst have
  The blessings of the poor.

" Be thine a warm and open heart,
  Be thine unnumbered friends;
A life, held precious while it lasts,
  And wept for when it ends.

And, heaven on earth, be thine a home
  Where children round thee grow,
Where one, with all thy mother's love,
  Makes blest thy days below.

"Harold, be thine that better life
  That higher still aspires,
Supreme in sovereign sway above
  The senses' low desires;
And thine the fame that, told of, men
  Of holy deeds shall hear,
A glory, unto good men's thoughts
  And lowly memories dear.

"Walk thou a poet among men,
  A prophet sent of God,
That hallowed grow the common ways
  Of earth, which thou hast trod;
That truth in thy eternal words
  Sit throned in might sublime,
And love and mercy, from thy tongue,
  For ever preach to Time.

" All human wishes most desire,
  All last they would resign,
All fondest love can long to give,
  My little one, be thine.
The purest good that man can know,
  To thee, my boy, be given;
And be thy every act on earth
  A deed, to win thee heaven !"

TO W. G. B.

SOUL, not yet from heaven beguiled,
  Soul, not yet by earth defiled,
Dwelling in this little child,
    Be, O to him be
    All we would have thee!

Through this life of joy and care,
If that grief must be his share,
Make, O make him strong to bear
    All God willeth, all
    That to him must fall.

O when passions stir his heart,
Tempting him from good to part,
Make him from the evil start,
    That he walk aright,
    Soil-less in God's sight!

Taint him not with mortal sin,
That heaven's palms his hands may win,
That heaven's gates he enter in,
    Of God's favour sure,
    Pure as he is pure!

If he wander from the right,
O through error's darksome night,
On to heaven's eternal light,
    Guide, O guide his way
    To heaven's perfect day!

CRADLE SONGS.

4.

SLEEP, boy, sleep—sleep!
  For the day is for waking—for rest the night,
And my boy must learn to use each aright;
      Let him toil in the day, and steep
Through the night his senses in slumber sound,
To fit him to work when day comes round!
      Sleep, boy, sleep—sleep!

      Sleep, boy, sleep—sleep!
For my boy must be strong of body and limb,
To do all I'd have to be done by him;
      Let his slumbers be sound and deep,
That stout of arm and of heart he may grow,
Both hot to do and keen to know;
      Sleep, boy, sleep—sleep!

      Sleep, boy, sleep—sleep!
For no puny son must I have—not I,
Made through his days but to crouch and sigh,
      To bend and to weakly weep;
No—my man must be strong to battle with care,
The bravest to do, and the boldest to dare;
      Sleep, boy, sleep—sleep!

      Sleep, boy, sleep—sleep!
Yes, thy mother, my boy, would have thee one
By whom this old world's best work is done;
      One who on its dullards shall sweep,   [strife,
If it must be, through storm—if it must be, through
To still freer thoughts, and to still purer life;
      Sleep, boy, sleep—sleep!

THE STORY OF A MOTHER.

FROM HANS CHRISTIAN ANDERSEN.

THERE the little one lay, white and dying,
  And beside its bed, with sorrow wild,
Wailed the mother, unto Heaven crying,
  " Spare my baby! spare, O God, my child!"

Then the darkness, death, arose before her,
  Laid its hand upon her baby's heart;
And, a nameless anguish creeping o'er her,
  From her infant saw she life depart.

It was dead, and fixed before her eye was
  That dear face that on her should have smiled;
But a moment dumb with grief, her cry was
  Straight, "O God! O give me back my child!"

Then it was as if God willed to send her
  Answer to the wail that from her rose;
And it seemed as if, with accents tender,   [close!"
  Death breathed, " Fate, what might have been, dis-

And with anguish that she might not smother,
  Looked she through the distant years with awe,
All the child had lived to, saw the mother;
  All its grown-up life the mother saw.

And she saw her babe, her heart's dear treasure,
   Fated, not to peace and joy, alas!
Fated, not to know a pure life's pleasure,
   But through want, and woe, and guilt to pass.

Then the mother knew her human blindness,
   And, even through her tears, she brightly smiled,
" Blessed be God !" she cried, " that in His kindness,
   Bore from earth, and sin, and shame, my child !"

CRADLE SONGS.

5.

SLEEP, baby, sleep!
  Cease thy bitter crying!
In the cold earth deep,
Deep in death's long sleep,
O that we were lying!
  Sleep, baby, sleep!

Sleep, baby, sleep!
Let's forget to-morrow
  Comes, when we must bear
  Scorn, and want, and care,
Waking but for sorrow!
  Sleep, baby, sleep!

Sleep, baby, sleep!
Thy poor mother pity!
  Worn and faint, she hears
  No voice her life that cheers
In all this great, hard city;
  Sleep, baby, sleep!

Sleep, baby, sleep!
Thou hast thy mother only;
  Cold and still lies he
  Who worked for thee and me,
And left us, boy, how lonely!
  Sleep, baby, sleep!

Sleep, baby, sleep!
Faint and, God! how weary!
Let these eyes, how blest!
Baby mine, in rest,
Forget this world so dreary!
Sleep, baby, sleep!

Sleep, baby, sleep!
Heed not mother's crying!
O boy, by God's will,
We were cold and still,
With thy father lying!
Sleep, baby, sleep!